T0004059

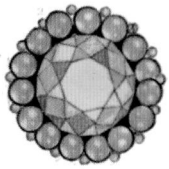

A Cache of Jewels

And Other Collective Nouns

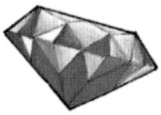

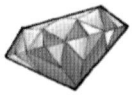

With

to
Richard P. Gross

PUFFIN BOOKS
Published by the Penguin Group
Penguin Group (USA) LLC
375 Hudson Street
New York, New York 10014

USA * Canada * UK * Ireland * Australia
New Zealand * India * South Africa * China

penguin.com
A Penguin Random House Company

First published in the United States of America by Grosset & Dunlap, 1987
Published by PaperStar, a registered trademark of The Putnam Berkley Group, Inc., 1998
Published by Puffin Books, an imprint of Penguin Young Readers Group, 2015

Copyright © 1987 by Ruth Heller

Penguin supports copyright. Copyright fuels creativity, encourages diverse voices, promotes free speech, and creates a vibrant culture. Thank you for buying an authorized edition of this book and for complying with copyright laws by not reproducing, scanning, or distributing any part of it in any form without permission. You are supporting writers and allowing Penguin to continue to publish books for every reader.

THE LIBRARY OF CONGRESS HAS CATALOGED THE GROSSET & DUNLAP EDITION AS FOLLOWS:
Heller, Ruth, date.
A cache of jewels : and other collective nouns / written and illustrated by Ruth Heller.
p. cm.
Summary: Rhyming text and illustrations introduce a variety of collective nouns such as a "drift of swans" and a "clutch of eggs."
ISBN 978-0-448-19211-6 (hardcover)
1. English language—Collective nouns—Juvenile literature. 2. English language—Terms and phrases—Juvenile literature. [1. English language—Prepositions. 2. English language—Terms and phrases.] I. Title.
PE1689 .H45 1987
428.1—dc20
87080254

Puffin Books ISBN 978-0-698-11354-1

Manufactured in China

30 29

A Cache of Jewels

And Other Collective Nouns

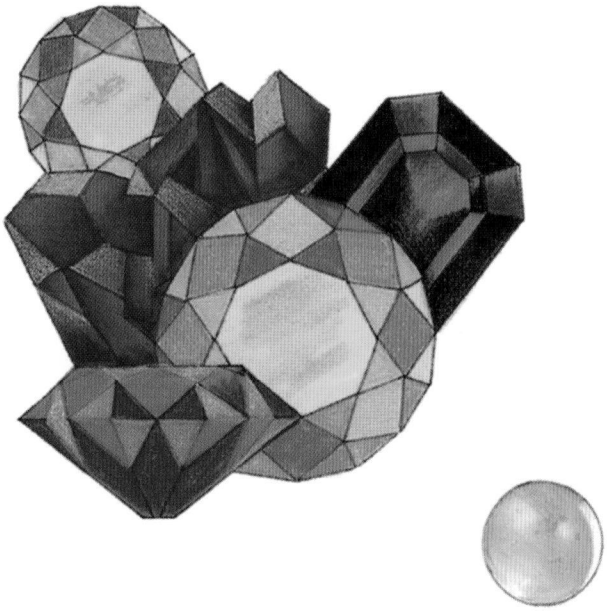

Written and illustrated by

RUTH HELLER

PUFFIN BOOKS
An Imprint of Penguin Group (USA)

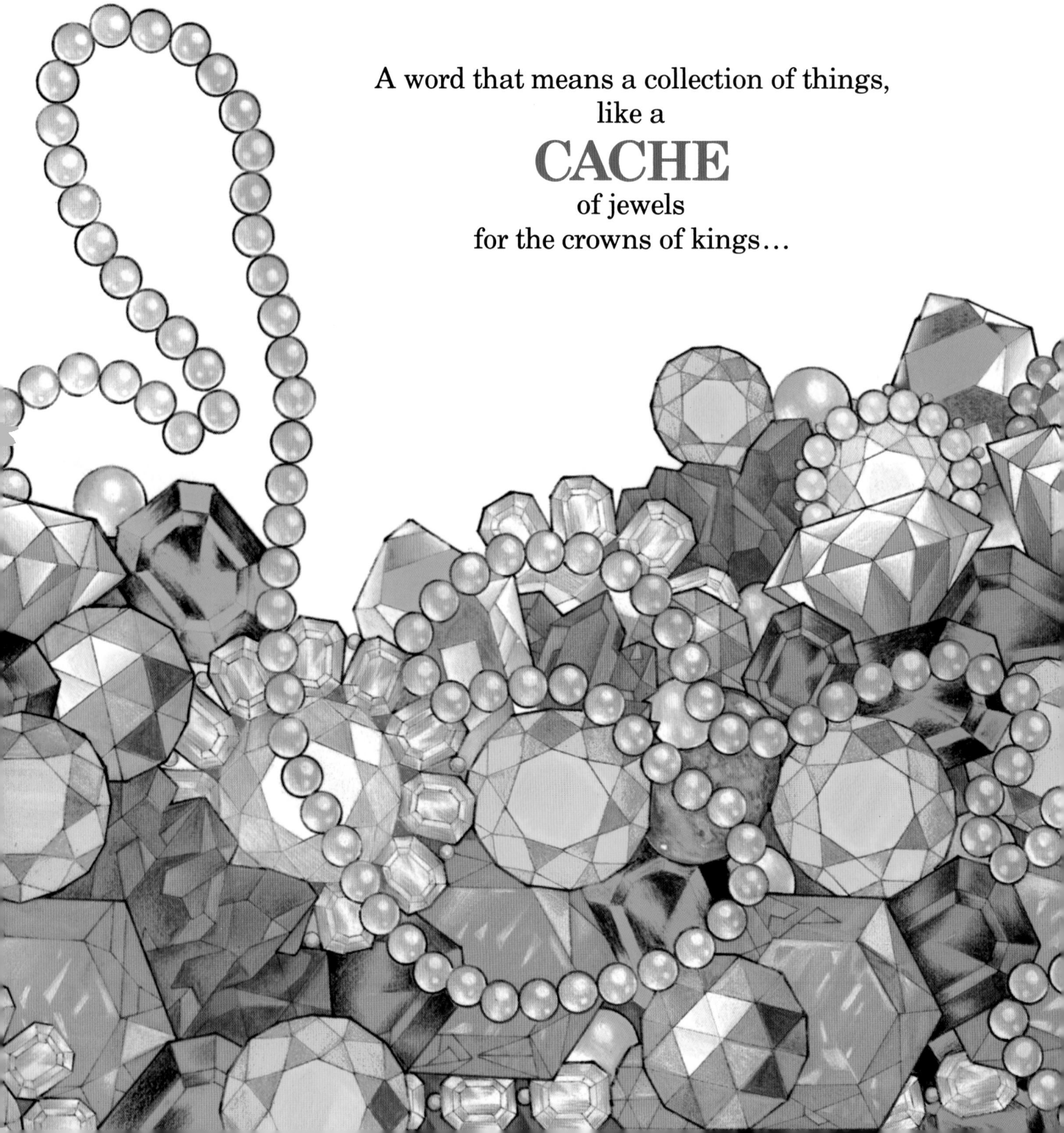

A word that means a collection of things,
like a
CACHE
of jewels
for the crowns of kings…

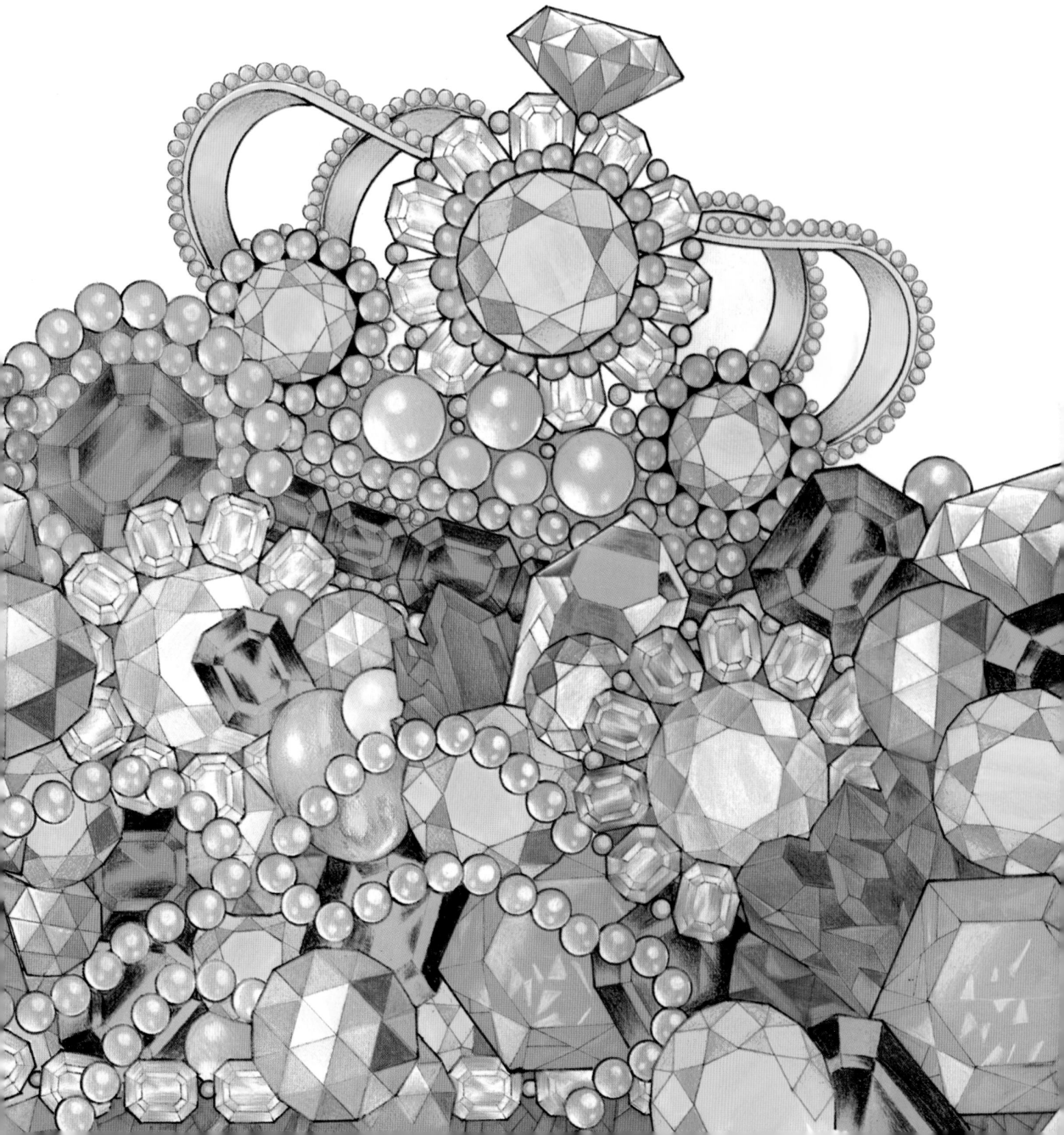

or a **BATCH** of bread all warm and brown,

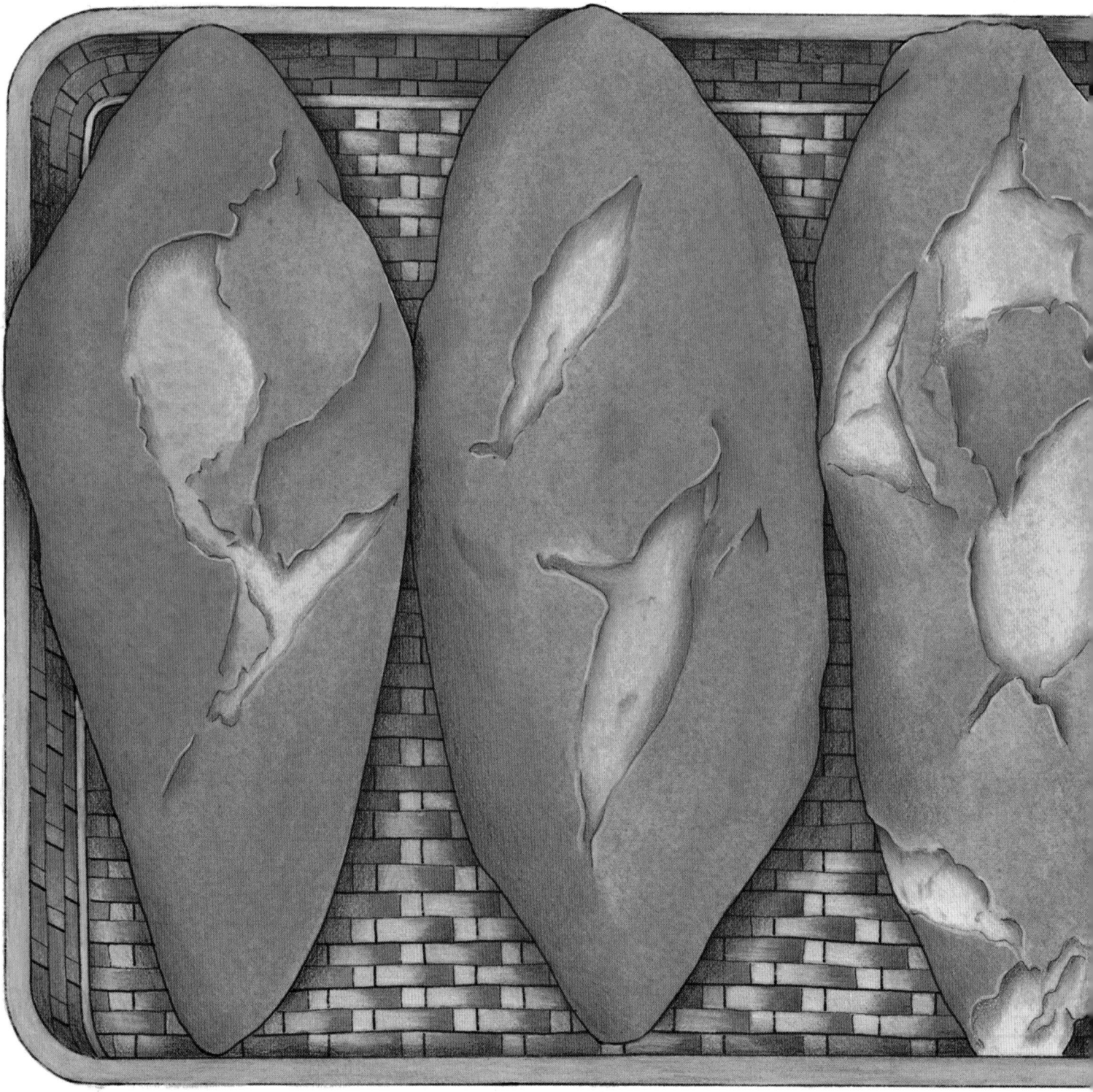

is always called a **COLLECTIVE NOUN**

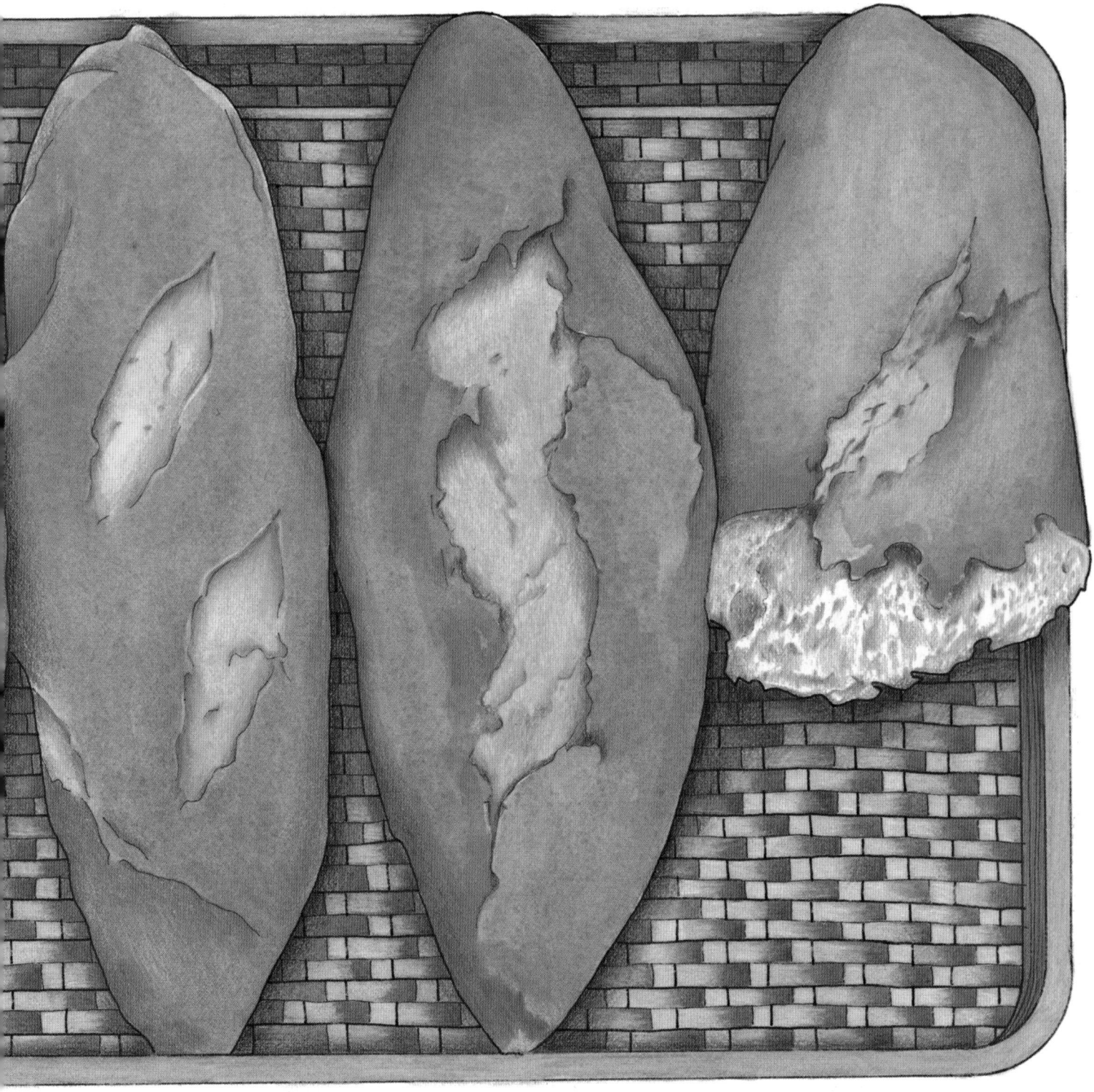

a SCHOOL of fish

a GAM of whales

a **FLEET** of ships
with
purple sails

a **BUNCH** of bananas

a
CLUSTER
of
grapes

a
BEVY
of
beauties
.
all different
shapes

a
MUSTER of peacocks

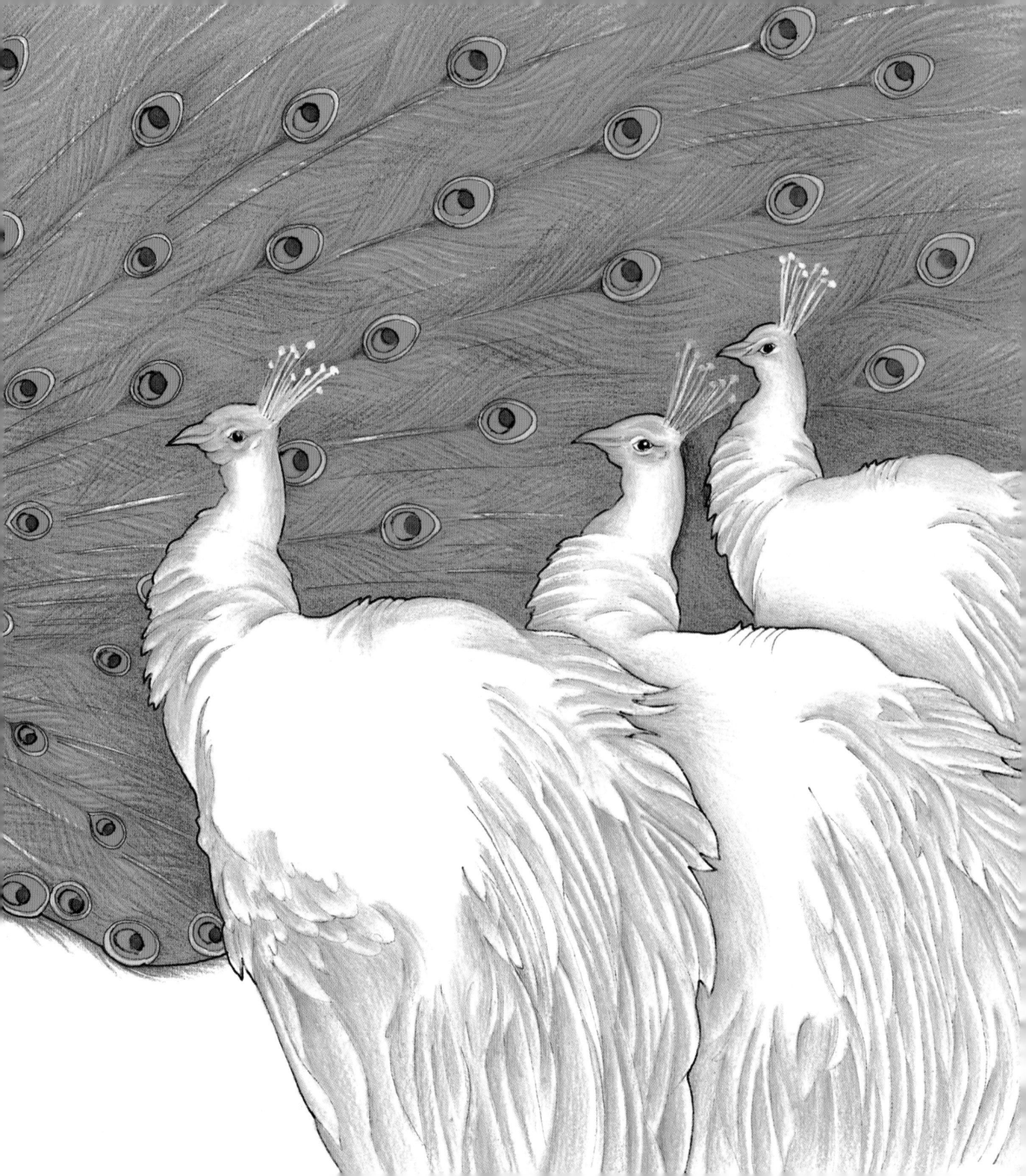

a
FLOCK
of
sheep

a
HOST
of
angels
fast
asleep

a BOUQUET
of flowers
a
SWARM
of
bees

a KINDLE of kittens
a
POD
of peas

a PARCEL of
penguins

a
FOREST
of
trees

a
COVEN
of
witches
as
scary
as
these

a **DRIFT** of swans

a **CLUMP**
of reeds

a
BED
of
oysters

a
STRING
of
beads

a
BROOD
of
chicks
a
CLUTCH
of
eggs

a
LITTER
of puppies on wobbly legs

a

PRIDE

of lions

a
LOCK
of hair

an
ARMY
of ants
from
here to…

there....

About five hundred years ago
knights and ladies in the know
used only very special words
to describe their flocks or herds.

These words are used by us today,
but some were lost along the way,
and new ones have been added too.

I've included quite a few.

And there are more of these group terms
like **sleuth** of bears
or **clew** of worms
or **rafter** of turkeys
walk of snails
leap of leopards
covey of quails.

But nouns aren't all collective,
and if I'm to be effective,
I'll tell about the other nouns
and adjectives and verbs.

All of them are parts of speech.

What fun!
I'll write a book for each.

—*Ruth Heller*

Note: One collective noun can describe many groups, as in a **host** of angels, daffodils, monks, thoughts, or sparrows.

One group can be described by more than one collective noun as in a **gam** of whales, a **mob** of whales, a **pod** of whales, a **school** of whales, or a **run** of whales.

Also Available by Ruth Heller